W9-BFA-322

3 1526 02897904 2

Double PINK

By Kate Feiffer

Illustrated by Bruce Ingman

A Paula Wiseman Book
Simon & Schuster Books for Young Readers
New York London Toronto Sydney

HARFORD COUNTY
PUBLIC LIBRARY
100 E. Pennsylvania Avenue
Bel Air, MD 21014

SIMON & SCHUSTER BOOKS FOR YOUNG READERS
An imprint of Simon & Schuster Children's Publishing Division
1230 Avenue of the Americas, New York, New York 10020
Text copyright © 2005 by Kate Feiffer
Illustrations copyright © 2005 by Bruce Ingman
All rights reserved, including the right of reproduction in whole or in part in any form.
SIMON & SCHUSTER BOOKS FOR YOUNG READERS is a trademark of Simon & Schuster, Inc.
Book design by Lucy Ruth Cummins
The text for this book is set in Garamond Infant.
The illustrations for this book are rendered in acrylic and ink.
Manufactured in China
10 9 8 7 6 5 4 3 2 1
Library of Congress Cataloging-in-Publication Data
Feiffer, Kate.
Double pink / Kate Feiffer ; illustrated by Bruce Ingman.—1st ed.
p. cm.
"A Paula Wiseman book."
Summary: Madison covers and surrounds herself with her favorite color, pink,
until the day her mother has trouble finding her.
ISBN-13: 978-0-689-87190-0
ISBN-10: 0-689-87190-2
[1. Color—Fiction.] I. Ingman, Bruce, 1963- ill. II. Title.
PZ7.F33346Do 2005
[E]—dc22
2004006582

WITHDRAWN

To Madeline—K. F.
To Alvie—B. I.

When Madison was a baby, her parents
waited for her to say her first word.

They waited
and they waited.

And then, after they waited a
little while longer, Madison said:

PINK!

From that day on, Madison loved pink. She loved pink more than blue, yellow, or orange. In fact, Madison loved pink more than all the colors in the rainbow. Pink was perfect. It was just so very, very pink.

CIRQUE D'HIVER
L'HOMME OBUS

Madison loved pink so much that she asked her mother to buy her the pinkest dress she could find.

Madison looked at almost pink and nearly pink dresses; dresses with pink stripes, pink polka dots, and pink flowers; dresses in bubble-gum pink, tickle-me pink, and princess pink. And then she pointed to a dress so perfectly pink that it was double pink.

Madison loved pink so much that she asked her mother for pink tights, pink shoes, a pink headband, and pink sunglasses to wear with her new double-pink dress.

Madison wore her pink dress with her pink tights, pink shoes, pink headband, and pink sunglasses every single hour of every single day.

When Madison's mother asked her if she wanted a glass of milk, Madison said, "Only if it's pink." So Madison's mother made her pink milk. It tasted like strawberries. Madison slurped it down. Madison wanted to paint the walls of her room pink. She asked her mother for pink walls. Her mom said, "Okay."

While the painters were painting Madison's walls, she asked them to paint her ceiling pink too. They said, "Okay." Soon Madison had pink walls and a pink ceiling.

But her pink walls and pink ceiling were lonely without a pink bedspread, pink sheets, and a pink pillow. So Madison got a pink bedspread, pink sheets, and a pink pillow.

Madison looked down at her blue rug and thought, *If only I had a pink rug.* "Please, Mama," she said, "can I have a pink rug?"

Then Madison decided she only wanted pink toys, and so she gave away all her stuffed animals that weren't pink. She kept her pink bear, her pink bunny, her pink turtle, and her three pink flamingos.

On her birthday Madison gave all her friends pink party hats, and they played Pin the Pink on the Rainbow. Madison's grandmother gave her a pink table and pink chairs. And Madison's best friend, Julie, gave her pink Magic Markers and pink paint. Of course, all her presents were wrapped in pink wrapping paper.

When it was time to blow out the pink candles on her pink cake, Madison wished that everything in the world was pink. Or even double pink.

When Madison's teacher announced Wear Your Favorite Color to School Day, Madison was ready. She put on all her pink clothes. She wore so much pink that she looked double pink, maybe even triple pink. Madison won a blue ribbon for all her pink and got her picture on the front page of the newspaper. The picture was printed in black and white.

One day when Madison's mother was busy in the other room, Madison put on pink lipstick and a pink wig. Then she colored her face and hands pink.

"Mama," she called, "come see me."
Madison's mother stopped doing whatever it was that she was doing without Madison and walked into Madison's room, but all she could see was pink.

Where was Madison?
"Madison," she said, "where are you?"

Think

Pink!

"I'm right here," said Madison.

Madison's mother walked over to the voice and picked up her daughter. But it wasn't Madison she picked up. It was a pink bear.

"That's not me," said Madison.

"I'm right here."

"Oh," said her mother, and she picked up a pink chair. "Is this you?"

"No," said Madison. "I'm here!"

"I think I see you now," said her mother, and she picked up a pink pillow.

"NOOO!!!!" yelled Madison. "I'm here!" Madison threw her arms in the air and waved them around.

"Now I see you," said her mother assuredly. But instead of picking up Madison, she picked up the pink table.

Madison jumped up, hopped to the left, and twirled seven times to the right. "Did you see that?" she asked.

"All I see is pink," lamented her mother.

Madison looked around. Everything
was pink. Everything was double pink.
Everything was too pink.

Too pink?

Yes, too pink!

Where had all the colors gone?

Madison searched for a patch of purple, but there was none. She tried to find a bit of blue, but there was none. She couldn't find a dab of brown, a dot of orange, or a smidgen of silver. There was not a stripe of yellow or a splash of green to be seen.

She missed them.

She missed her brown bear and her red fire truck. She missed her green balloon and her favorite *not*-pink shoes—which were blue.

ding
ding

Then Madison had an idea.

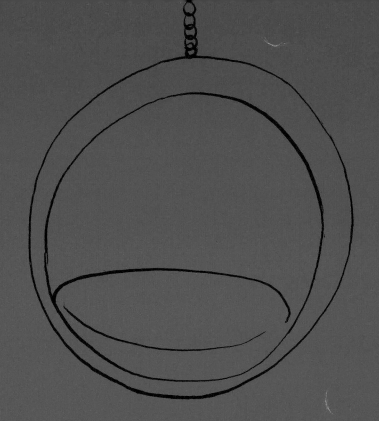

She got her pink eraser and started to erase. But the pink paint on her walls didn't erase. The pink on her bedspread didn't erase. The pink on her pink toys didn't erase, and the pink on her shoes didn't erase.

Madison's mother asked, "Madison, are you still in here?"

Think ----- Pink!

"Yes," Madison said, and started to cry—but only for a second or two, because after a second or two a tear washed away a line of pink. Then another tear washed away a circle of pink. Then another circle and another line washed away and . . .

There was Madison.

"I'm so glad I found you!" said her mother.

Madison's mother picked up Madison and gave her two great big kisses. They were red. Double red.

Madison loved red. . . .